Boonoonoonous Hair!

To Helene —OS

For Neville, Zuri and Mennen, with all my love—LJ

Published by Tradewind Books in Canada and the UK in 2019
Text copyright © 2019 Olive Senior • Illustrations copyright © 2019 Laura James

All rights reserved. No part of this publication may be reproduced, stored in a retrieval system or transmitted, in any form or by any means, without the prior written permission of the publisher or, in the case of photocopying or other reprographic copying, a license from Access Copyright, Toronto, Ontario. The right of Olive Senior and Laura James to be identified as the author and the illustrator of this work has been asserted by them in accordance with the Copyright, Design and Patents Act 1988.

Book design by Elisa Gutiérrez

The text of this book is set in Grenale Slab. The title is Mr Hyde from YWFT

10   9   8   7   6   5   4   3   2   1

. . . .

LIBRARY AND ARCHIVES CANADA CATALOGUING IN PUBLICATION

Senior, Olive, author
Boonoonoonous hair / Olive Senior ; illustrations by Laura James.

ISBN 978-1-926890-07-4 (hardback)

I. James, Laura, 1971-, illustrator II. Title.

PS8587.E552B66 2016   jC813.6   C2016-905395-4

. . . .

Printed and bound
in Korea on ancient
forest-friendly paper.

The publisher thanks the Government of Canada, the Canada Council for the Arts and Livres Canada Books for their financial support. We also thank the Government of the Province of British Columbia for the financial support it has given through the Book Publishing Tax Credit program and the British Columbia Arts Council.

OLIVE SENIOR

Boonoonoonous Hair!

Illustrations by
LAURA JAMES

TRADEWIND BOOKS
Vancouver • London

Time to plait Jamilla's hair,
   but the comb has vanished into thin air.

It's up in the ceiling, Jamilla shouts.
The elephant's hiding it in his trunk.

O really! Last time it was the camel's hump.

The kangaroo's pouch.
The toucan's beak.
The mouse's squeak.

Now Missy, no more playing.
Spin around and let's get braiding.
Aha! Look where the comb's been hiding.

Waaah! Jamilla cries.

Oh come now, Jamilla, this is no time to pout.
You'll be late for school unless I comb it out—
Close your eyes. Count to ten.
I'll be done with this plait by then.

I hate my hair. It hurts. It's a pain.

O do stop making such a fuss.
Why do you hate your hair so much?

Because it's bad, bad, bad.
Makes me so mad, mad, mad.

Why can't I have good hair
like the girls in my class—
Sasha, Sarah, Brittany, Claire?

Oh really, what's so good about their hair?

They have hair that's long and soft
and pretty. It glows as it flows
without plaits without pins,
long or short
it can swish as they wish.

O Jamilla, you silly, why want
their hair, when the most
fantabulous,
splendiferous,
boonoonoonous hair
in the world
is right here?

Really?

And truly, you'll see. Your hair
is electric, kinetic and free.
While your friends' hair always
looks the same, you have hair
that can frame your face or
whizz off into the stratosphere.
Hair that can say something
different every day of the week,
every month of the year.
Want to try?

Oh yes, a different head of hair
every day of the year?

Well . . . let's start with this week.

So I can have puffs on Monday . . .

Plaits on Tuesday . . .

Braids on Wednesday . . .

Cornrows Thursday . . .

Twist out Friday?

Yes, and on
Saturday hair
can be wild.

But on Sunday you must be Grandmother's child.

But guess what? No more hiding the comb.
No more crying. Agree?

Uh-huh, boo-noo-noo-nous!

And boonoonoonous you!
For the first day of school
Here's your new do.

Now, promise Jamilla—
No hiding the comb.
No getting in a tizzy.

Sometimes Mom might be busy,
So ask Big Sister Lizzy.

Coz, she's been there?

With her electric, kinetic,
Bombastic, fantastic . . .

Twirly, whirly, curly, fuzzy, snappy, nappy,
Wavy, crazy . . .

onous hair!